Dear mouse friends,
Welcome to the world of

Geronimo Stilton

THE RODENT'S GAZETTE
EDITORIAL STAFF

Geronimo Stilton
A learned and brainy
mouse; editor of
The Rodent's Gazette

Thea Stilton
Geronimo's sister and
special correspondent at
The Rodent's Gazette

Trap Stilton
An awful joker;
Geronimo's cousin and
owner of the store
Cheap Junk for Less

Benjamin Stilton
A sweet and loving
nine-year-old
mouse; Geronimo's
favorite nephew

Geronimo *Stilton*

THE HUNT FOR THE
COLOSSEUM GHOST

PLUS a bonus
Mini Mystery and
cheesy jokes!

Scholastic Inc.

Pages i–111; 194–198 copyright © 2016 by Edizioni Piemme S.p.A., Palazzo Mondadori, Via Mondadori 1, 20090 Segrate, Italy. International Rights © Atlantyca S.p.A. English translation © 2018 by Atlantyca S.p.A.

Pages 112–193 copyright © 2008 by Edizioni Piemme S.p.A., Palazzo Mondadori, Via Mondadori 1, 20090 Segrate, Italy. International Rights © Atlantyca S.p.A. English translation © 2015 by Atlantyca S.p.A.

Published by Scholastic Inc., *Publishers since 1920*, 557 Broadway, New York, NY 10012. SCHOLASTIC and associated logos are trademarks and/or registered trademarks of Scholastic Inc.

Library of Congress Cataloging-in-Publication Data available

ISBN 978-1-338-21522-9

Pages i–111
Text by Geronimo Stilton
Original title *Il fantasma del Colosseo*
Cover by Roberto Roch and Andrea Carallini
Illustrations by Danilo Loizedda, Antonio Campo, and Daria Cerchi
Graphics by Michela Battaglin and Chiara Cebrais

Special thanks to AnnMarie Anderson
Translated by Anna Pizzelli
Interior design by Kay Petronio

Pages 112–193
Text by Geronimo Stilton
Original title *Il ladro di croste*
Cover by Giuseppe Ferrario and Giulia Zaffaroni
Illustrations by Andrea Denegri (pencils and inks) and Daria Cerchi (color)
Graphics by Michael Battaglin and Marta Lorini
Fingerprint graphic © NREY/Shutterstock
Special thanks to Beth Dunfey
Translated by Anna Pizzelli
Interior design by Becky James

10 9 8 7 6 5 4 3 2 1   18 19 20 21 22

Printed in China   38
First edition, April 2018

Table of Contents

THE HUNT FOR THE COLOSSEUM GHOST

A STRANGE, CHEESE-COLORED ENVELOPE . . .

I had just arrived at my office for the day when my assistant, Mousella Mac Mouser, dumped a HUGE pile of mail on my desk.

Here you go!

So much mail!

Oh, I'm sorry! I forgot to introduce myself. My name is Stilton, *Geronimo Stilton*, and I am the publisher of *The Rodent's Gazette*, the most famous newspaper on Mouse Island.

As I was saying, I had a lot of mail: one envelope contained a **contract** to sign, another held a *manuscript* by a promising new writer, and one was a postcard my aunt Sweetfur had sent from her vacation on Furflung Island. There were also bills to pay: the office's gas bill, a bill from my architect friend Mousilina Straightedge (she had recently installed solar panels on my house), and a bill from the mechanic who had just fixed my car. Finally, there was a *purple, perfumed envelope*.

Squeak! I immediately recognized the scent: it was **Ratell No. 5**, my friend Creepella von Cacklefur's favorite perfume!

One thing you should know is that Creepella

tells everyone she is my *girlfriend*, but it's not true. We're just friends, rodent's honor! I *opened* the envelope:

Gerrykins, next week is our anniversary! I have planned a cheese stew dinner at Cacklefur Castle with the whole family. Don't forget!

—Your beloved Creepella

"what anniversary?" I squeaked aloud. "We aren't even dating!"

Crusty kitty litter, a dinner at Cacklefur Castle with the whole family? I can't stand cheese stew! And Creepella's family can be incredibly . . . well, creepy!

I was about to call Creepella to let her know once and for all that I only like her as a friend. I also planned to tell her I couldn't attend an anniversary party with her entire family. But then I caught sight of an official-looking yellow letter in the stack of mail . . .

What a strange, cheese-colored envelope!

I opened it immediately and almost jumped out of my fur in surprise.

Holey cheese, it was a letter from the principal at my little nephew Benjamin's school! I remembered Mr. Strictfur well; he had been my teacher long ago.

For a moment, I took a trip down memory lane: Mr. Strictfur had been my history teacher at Little Tails Academy. My fellow students and I were always so nervous whenever there was a quiz; it's no coincidence that his name is Strictfur!

Dear Mr. Stilton,

I am writing to inform you that your nephew Benjamin Stilton is struggling to keep his grades up this semester. His history grade is especially problematic. In fact, his teacher recently quizzed him on ancient Rome and he was not able to answer a single question correctly! Let me know when we can meet to discuss this issue. Benjamin is a very bright young mouselet, and I would like to give him a chance to improve his grades before it's too late. I don't want to have to hold him back at the end of the school year!

Best regards,

Stuart Strictfur

Principal

He was one of the toughest teachers in the school, but years later, I understand that it was because he cared about us. It's thanks to him that I learned so many things about **history** that have been useful in my job at *The Rodent's Gazette*. And now history was the very subject that seemed to be causing Benjamin the most **trouble**!

STRICTFUR'S AMAZING MEMORY

I picked up my phone and IMMEDIATELY called the principal.

"Hello?" I squeaked. "Am I speaking to Mr. Stuart Strictfur?"

"Stilton? Geronimo Stilton?" a **Deep** voice replied. "Is it really you? The ONE who always sat in the back of the class? The one who used to throw spitballs at the mouselet with GOLDEN BRAIDS who sat in the third desk on the right in the second row? The one who could never remember when ROME was founded? The one I was about to hold back in fifth grade because he was always daydreaming instead of **STUDYING**? *That* Geronimo Stilton?"

I was flabbergasted!

Holey cheese, what an excellent memory! He had recognized me by my voice, and he had remembered everything about me, down to the mouselet I had a crush on . . .

"Uh, yes, Mr. Strictfur, it's me, *Stilton, Geronimo Stilton*. I can't believe you still remember me."

"Are you kidding, Stilton?" he replied with a chuckle. "**Stuart Strictfur** never forgets a **SNOUT**, a **name**, or a **grade**!"

Gulp! Was it possible he really remembered my terrible history grade?

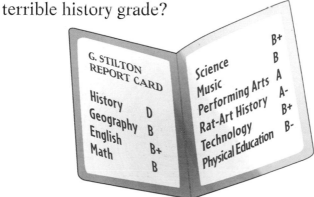

G. STILTON
REPORT CARD

History   D
Geography   B
English   B
Math   B+
               B

Science   B+
Music   B
Performing Arts A
Rat-Art History A-
Technology   B+
Physical Education B-

"I remember perfectly well that you **struggled** with history until I got you to improve," he continued. "Do you remember when I took the class to Rome on a **SCHOOL TRIP**? You started doing pretty well right after that. In fact, your history grade that year was an **A**!"

"Yes, you're right!" I agreed. "Thank you for taking me on that trip."

I recalled how much that visit had **changed** my outlook on history. Mr. Strictfur had helped me learn to **love** and appreciate the past. I could still recall him tearing up as he stood outside the **Colosseum** and told our class about its historical significance.

"Gladiators fought in this arena, Romans sat on these steps, and **ROME'S** most popular shows took place here," Mr. Strictfur had squeaked **PASSIONATELY**.

"Close your eyes and pretend you've gone back

in time. Imagine you see the senators and the emperor surrounded by his trusted men. Now pretend you can smell the bread the Romans loved to eat, and pretend you can hear the cheering crowd. History isn't dead — it's alive, and it's fabumouse! Studying history is just like traveling through time!"

From then on, history had become my favorite subject.

Suddenly, I had a revelation.

"Principal Strictfur, I was just calling to

Gladiators fought in this arena!

let you know that you don't have to WORRY about my nephew Benjamin's history grade. I'm going to help him improve it by doing what you did with me years ago:

I'm taking him on a trip to Rome!"

Then I hung up the phone and called Benjamin right away.

"Hi, Nephew!" I squeaked. "I know you're having a hard time in school right now, but don't worry. I'll help you learn all about ancient Rome, and we'll do it while having fun! We're going to VISIT Rome together, and soon you'll have a much easier time remembering all the most important historical events that happened there. Your cousin Trappy will join us, too. Pack your bags — we're leaving in the morning!"

The next day, the three of us were on our way to

Rome. We boarded a special **nonstop flight** to Italy that included unlimited pizza throughout the entire trip. 𝕐𝕌𝕄!

Trappy is Benjamin's cousin and his good friend. She looks a lot like Trap!

A GUIDE TO ROME

Italy is a country in south-central Europe that is shaped like a boot and has a long coastline on the Mediterranean Sea.

The capital of Italy is Rome, a city with more than 2,800,000 residents. The earliest Roman settlements were built on seven hills. This busy city is full of monuments and archeological ruins, including the famous Colosseum, the Sistine Chapel, the Pantheon, and the Spanish Steps.

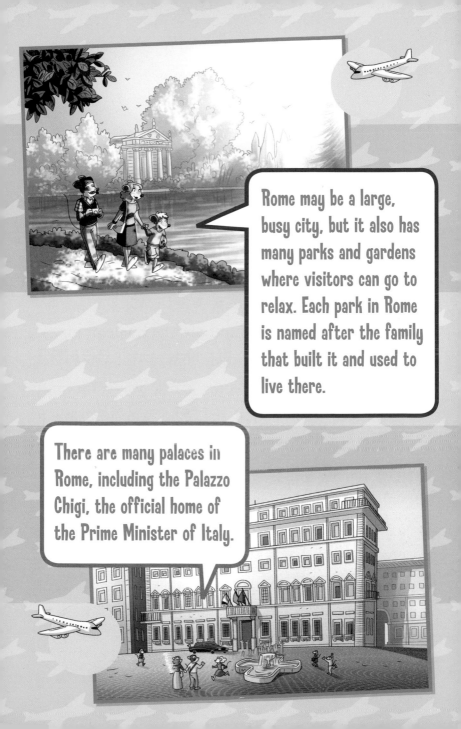

Rome may be a large, busy city, but it also has many parks and gardens where visitors can go to relax. Each park in Rome is named after the family that built it and used to live there.

There are many palaces in Rome, including the Palazzo Chigi, the official home of the Prime Minister of Italy.

DON'T YOU RECOGNIZE ME?

As soon as we landed, we collected our luggage. While we were waiting for a taxi to take us to downtown Rome, I **DEVOURED** a triple-cheese pizza. We were in Italy, the home of pizza, and I couldn't help myself! I was still **eating** when a rodent with long, dark, wavy fur and dark eyes approached me. She was wearing a **cheese-colored** pantsuit, and she gave me a big hug.

"Um, hello?" I squeaked.

"Geronimo!" She gasped dramatically. "Don't you *recognize* me?"

I had no idea who she was! Also, the bite of pizza I had just **SWALLOWED** was stuck in my throat.

"Uh, hmmmm . . ." I replied.

She giggled.

"Come on, I'm Ratella Spywhiskers!" she said, winking at me. "You remember me now, don't you? You haven't **changed** one bit. Always stuffing yourself with **pizza**, you foodie!"

Then she *winked* at me again.

"Uh, no, sorry . . ." I mumbled.

"Ger, how could you forget me?" she squeaked, annoyed this time. "We were in the same class at New Mouse City High School. See, look at this picture."

She winked at me a **third** time and then waved a **photo** in front of my snout. It showed me and another mouse sitting at two desks, but the rodent in the photo looked **nothing like her**!

She had written on the photo in red marker:

Wake up! Pretend you recognize me, Special Agent 00G! I am Special Agent

OOR! You have just been recruited for a very secret mission in Rome!

I should tell you that sometimes I work as a secret agent for the government of Mouse Island, and that my secret agent name is **OOG**.

"Holey cheese!" I squeaked in reply. "Of course I **recognize** you . . . er . . . Ratella! It's been such a *long* time since I last saw you!

"You just look so **DIFFERENT** than you did when we attended school together," I babbled on. "I mean, of course you're the same **MOUSE**. How could I forget you?"

Benjamin reached out to shake her paw.

"Pleased to meet you, Miss Spywhiskers," he said sweetly.

Trappy giggled.

How could you forget me?

Of course I recognize you!

HERE IS THE STORY OF HOW I BECAME SECRET AGENT *OOG* . . .

During my first mission as a secret agent for the government of Mouse Island, I worked with agents OOK and OOV to prevent the theft of the solid gold, diamond-studded Super Mouse Cup. The trophy is the prize for the annual champion of the Mouseport Golf Tournament.

Then, when the scientist Dr. Wicked Whiskers threatened New Mouse City, I was sent on a space mission with agents OOK and OOV to uncover his evil plan, and we managed to protect Mouse Island once again!

KORNELIUS VON KICKPAW

Name: Kornelius von Kickpaw

Code Name: ooK

Profession: Secret agent for the government of Mouse Island

Who he is: Geromino's friend from elementary school

Accessories: He always wears a super-accessorized tuxedo and sunglasses, even at night.

VERONICA VON KICKPAW

Name: Veronica von Kickpaw

Special Agent: ooV

Profession: Secret agent for the government of Mouse Island

Who she is: Agent ooK's sister

Distinguishing Marks: She always wears a mysterious, unique, and unmistakable perfume.

"You were Uncle G's classmate?" she asked, astonished. "**WOW!** How FUNNY that we bumped into you here!"

Ratella winked at me again.

"Where are you staying, Geronimo?" she asked.

"At the **Three Tails Hotel**," I replied.

"What a LUCKY coincidence!" she squeaked. "I'm staying there, too!"

So we all shared a **TAXI** to the hotel. When we arrived a SHORT time later, we sat down to eat another mouserific pizza!

While I was *gobbling up* the last slice, my cell phone rang.

It was my grandfather, William Shortpaws. He's the original founder of *The Rodent's Gazette*, and he's always keeping tabs on me.

"Grandson!" he shouted into the phone. "What's this I hear about you taking a trip to Italy? Thanks to my slacker alarm, I just knew you weren't working! Get back to the paper right away!"

"Well, Grandfather," I tried to explain, "there's a good reason why I'm here, and it involves **BENJAMIN**. And as a publisher and editor, it's good for me to travel and expose myself to new ideas and the latest news."

"New ideas? Latest news?" Grandfather huffed. "Well, in my opinion, you're just slacking off, as usual! And I'm sure you're **STUFFING** yourself with pizza, too!"

Holey cheese,

What a slacker!

The **slacker alarm** is a very complicated alarm system that Grandfather William invented. He mainly uses it to keep tabs on me and to let me know when he thinks I'm slacking off.

how does Grandfather always know **exactly** what's going on? I hung up the phone and picked up a newspaper so I would feel a little less **guilty** about being away from work. I glanced at the **headlines**.

Chewy cheddar, what a **shock**:

Is it true? What?

SOMEONE WANTED TO BUY THE COLOSSEUM!

BREAKING NEWS

SOMEONE WANTS TO BUY THE COLOSSEUM!

by Ned Nosysnout

According to local sources, a mysterious rodent from Mouse Island wants to buy one of the most important and well-known monuments in the world: the Roman Colosseum.

No one knows the identity of the mysterious rodent, who arrived in Rome disguised in a large leopard-print hat, a leopard-print raincoat, and dark sunglasses. But thanks to this intrepid reporter's hard work, here is an exclusive interview with her!

"Yes, it's true: I want to buy the Colosseum," she told us, "But I'm not interested in old, crumbling monuments. I plan to tear it down with a bulldozer so I can build a luxurious apartment building with a large parking garage in its place! I love cement, don't you? Good riddance to ancient, decrepit ruins!"

THE COLOSSEUM GHOST

I headed to my hotel room **immediately**. There was a 🔒S🔒U🔒I🔒T🔒C🔒A🔒S🔒E🔒 in the closet with a card inside it:

Secret-Agent Suitcase
(especially for secret missions in Italy)
Secret Agent OOG,
Your mission in Rome is to find out why there is a

GHOST HAUNTING THE COLOSSEUM.

Good luck!
(You'll need it!)

"A ghost is haunting the Colosseum!" I squeaked. How furraising. I looked back into the suitcase. It contained:

1. A **tourist guide to Rome**, including a city map with detailed information on secret passageways and other information useful to a special agent

2.

3. A **small metallic box** containing one gray tablet that can create a thick smoke to shield me from my enemies

4. **Super-sticky glue**: stronger than concrete, stretchier than gum, and stickier than a thousand suction cups!

5. A **clothespin** (I had no idea what it was for!)

6. A **recipe** for secret-agent pizza

7. A **miniature gladiator costume**, complete with a thousand strange tools!

SECRET-AGENT SUITCASE

A TOURIST GUIDE TO ROME, INCLUDING A CITY MAP WITH DETAILED INFORMATION ON SECRET PASSAGEWAYS AND OTHER INFORMATION USEFUL TO A SPECIAL AGENT

STRANGE-LOOKING NIGHT VISION GOGGLES

A SMALL METALLIC BOX CONTAINING ONE GRAY TABLET THAT CAN CREATE A THICK SMOKE SHIELD

A CLOTHESPIN (WHO KNOWS WHY?)

A VACUUM-PACKED MINIATURE GLADIATOR COSTUME (FOR EMERGENCY USE ONLY!)

OOG
SECRET AGENT

A RECIPE FOR SECRET-AGENT PIZZA

PACKETS OF SUPER-STICKY GLUE: STRONGER THAN CONCRETE, STRETCHIER THAN GUM, AND STICKIER THAN A THOUSAND SUCTION CUPS!

THE SUITCASE TURNED INTO A BACKPACK THANKS TO TWO STRAPS ON THE BACK, AND THERE WAS ALSO AN UMBRELLA WITH AN INSTRUCTION MANUAL INSIDE.

Turn the page . . .

WARNING:
This looks like a normal umbrella, but it's not!

Features of the secret-agent UMBRELLA:

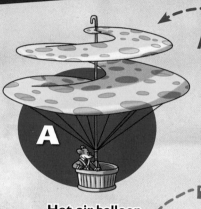

A) IT TURNS INTO A LIGHT AND STURDY FOUR-SEAT HOT-AIR BALLOON.

Hot-air-balloon umbrella

B) IT CAN LOCATE, DETECT, AND CAPTURE GHOSTS!

Ghost-catcher umbrella

C) IT GENERATES A POWERFUL MAGNETIC FIELD FOR UP TO FIVE MINUTES.

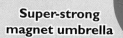

Super-strong magnet umbrella

D) IT CAN SHOOT OUT A LONG, STRONG STEEL CABLE WITH A HOOK AT THE END (HEY, YOU NEVER KNOW!).

Umbrella with cables

E) IT CAN TURN INTO A VERY POWERFUL FLASHLIGHT (IN CASE YOU END UP IN A CAVE).

Flashlight umbrella

F) IT CAN TURN INTO AN EMERGENCY RAFT IN CASE OF A SHIPWRECK!

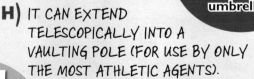

Raft umbrella

Hook umbrella

G) IT CAN BE USED AS A SIMPLE HOOK (FOR NOT-SO-SIMPLE ESCAPES).

Pole-vault umbrella

H) IT CAN EXTEND TELESCOPICALLY INTO A VAULTING POLE (FOR USE BY ONLY THE MOST ATHLETIC AGENTS).

I) IT CAN BE USED AS AN EMERGENCY SHIELD FOR ANYTHING AND EVERYTHING!

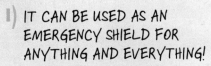

Emergency-shield umbrella

"Pole vault?" I mumbled to myself. "**No way** — not for all the pizza in Rome. I am **not** an athletic mouse!"

I used the two straps to turn the suitcase into a B A C K P A C K . Then I put the umbrella back in the bag and pulled it onto my shoulders.

A second later, my cell phone rang:

RING RING RING!

It was Ratella Spywhiskers.

A ghost?!

"Secret Agent 00G," she squeaked, "come down to the main lobby **immediately**. Listen to my instructions very carefully: we are going to pretend to be regular tourists visiting the Colosseum. We'll try to take an official tour, but it won't be easy.

"Apparently a ghost has been **SCARING** tourists away for at least a week. Now come on down — I'll wait for you here. By the way, this **MISSION** is extremely dangerous. But you're not scared, are you?"

"N-no, no," I stuttered. "Of course not!"

But my whiskers were **trembling** with fear as I **went downstairs** with Benjamin and Trappy, feeling very anxious.

Why, oh why had I ever agreed to become a secret agent?

You're not scared, are you?

A SCREAM AT SUNSET

We had just enough time to grab a quick *vegetarian* pizza at the hotel before we hopped on a bus to start our tour of the city.

The guide was pointing out the most interesting and well-known sites.

"That's the Roman Forum on our left, the center of **ancient Roman** public life.

"Over there are the remains of the *Domus*

Aurea, also called the 'Golden House.' The ornate palace had high gold ceilings decorated with *precious* stones and was the home of Emperor Nero. And to the right are the ruins of some ancient Roman baths, where everyone went daily to bathe, relax, and socialize. If you head in that direction, you'll find the oldest Roman road, the Appian Way."

"Old roads? Ancient baths? Wow!" Benjamin squeaked with **delight**. "Can you tell me who

Uncle G, this is fabumouse!

This is the Porta San Paolo and there's the Pyramid of Cestius!

THE FABUMOUSE CITY OF
ROME

This is the **Castel Sant'Angelo**. It was built by the emperor Hadrian as a mausoleum for his family, but was later used by different popes as a fortress and castle.

Here is the **Trevi Fountain**, one of the oldest water sources in Rome. It's built mainly from travertine stone, one of the same materials used to construct the Colosseum.

The **Appian Way** is considered the world's first highway. It is the road that connects Rome to the city of Brindisi, which in ancient times was the most important port used to sail for Greece, the Middle East, and Asia.

Trajan's Column was built to commemorate Emperor Trajan's two victories over the Dacians, a civilization in modern-day Romania, in 101 and 106 CE.

The Roman Forum was the central meeting place for all Roman citizens. It was the place where they discussed political, economic, and religious matters.

The Baths of Caracalla was one of the places ancient Romans could go daily to bathe, exercise, play, meet friends, and relax. It is still standing today, and many mosaics inside the building are partially visible.

The Colosseum (also called the Flavian Amphitheater) is one of Rome's most famous sites!

built them and when? You were right, Uncle G — history is mouserific!"

I smiled. My plan was **working**: Benjamin was becoming more interested in **history**!

"Uncle G, look!" Trappy squeaked suddenly. She pointed to a very **long** leopard-print car that seemed to be following us. **How strange!**

It looked exactly like Madame No's car. But what was she doing here in Rome? Before I could figure it out, we pulled up in front of the Colosseum.

Come on, let's go!

I'm scared! I heard there's a ghost!

Huh?

When I got off the bus, I saw the *fancy* leopard-print car with tinted windows again. It was parked right outside the Colosseum.

How strange!

"Ladies and gentlemice, our tour includes a VISIT to the Colosseum," our guide explained. "But no one has been inside since last week. It's said that a ghost is haunting the ruins . . ."

"Here are your **TICKETS**!" the ticket agent squeaked desperately.

"It's completely safe," the director of the Colosseum urged us kindly. "Please do come in!"

No way!

We'd better not!

Please, come on in!

MADAME NO

Name: Madame No

Job: CEO of EGO Corp (Enormousely Gigantic Organization), a powerful company with many subsidiaries that handles a lot of real-estate deals on Mouse Island. EGO Corp builds malls and skyscrapers and owns airlines, newspapers, and TV stations.

Distinguishing feature: Whenever you ask her a question, she will always answer with one word: "NO!"

Her passion: Automatic gadgets, robots, and drones that she has custom-made.

Her obsession: She is crazy about anything leopard print, from clothing to accessories to cars. She even owns a leopard-print limousine.

Her slogan: "I always win, no matter what, and no matter how!"

Her secret: Madame No is the trusted assistant to Mr. Mystery, a sleazy rodent whose identity is unknown, but whose dirty deals are polluting Mouse Island.

Her dream: To become the richest and most powerful rodent on Mouse Island.

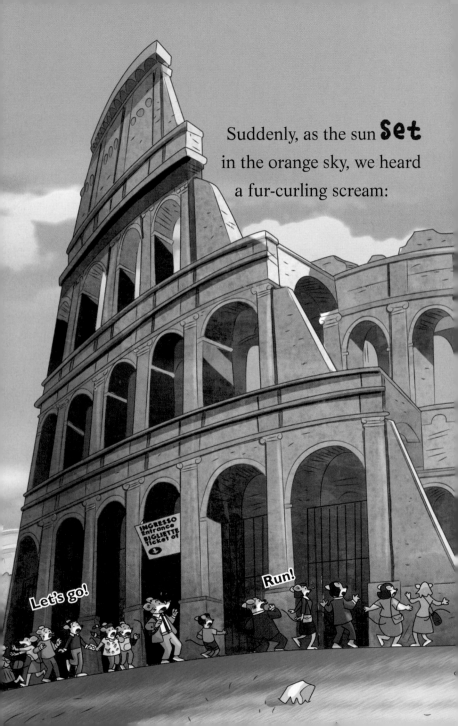

NED AND EARL
NOSYSNOUT

Trappy and Benjamin looked up at me fearfully.

"My whiskers are shaking, Uncle!" Trappy squeaked softly.

"Anyone would be **SCARED**," Ratella Spywhiskers whispered. "But not you, Secret Agent 00G, right?"

My teeth were chattering in terror, but I tried to get ahold of myself.

"O-of course n-n-not," I stammered. "I'm n-not **S-SCARED** at a-all . . ."

At that moment, I spied an arrogant-looking rat near the entrance to the Colosseum. I recognized him immediately: it was NED NOSYSNOUT, a famouse reporter from Mouse Island!

I didn't know him personally, but I knew he

had a reputation for being **RUTHLESS**: he would do **ANYTHING** to get an exclusive story!

He recognized me, too.

"Well, well," he said with a smirk. "It's *Geronimo Stilton*, in the fur. What are you doing here?"

I smiled. "That's right, it's me," I replied. "I came to Rome to visit the **COLOSSEUM**."

"You can't go inside the Colosseum!" he said with a dramatic gasp. "They say it's haunted by a **VERY DANGEROUS** ghost!"

Ned Nosysnout: Famouse reporter

Earl Nosysnout: Cameramouse

Then he turned to his cameramouse, Earl (who is also his cousin).

"But the two of us are planning to go inside anyway," Ned boasted. "And when we come out, we'll have the **best story of the year** ... no, of the **CENTURY**!"

"That's right, Ned," Earl replied with a sneer.

Meanwhile, the director of the Colosseum tried to reassure the tourists.

Wow! Cool! We will go in the Colosseum! Hmm ...

"There's really nothing to be afraid of," he insisted. "Please, you're all welcome to go inside!"

But no one else would go in. Instead, they clapped encouragingly for Ned and Earl.

"You two are so **BRAVE**!" they shouted. "Way to go!"

So the two of them *boldly* walked inside. About five minutes later, they came running out, squeaking at the tops of their lungs!

They looked as pale as MOZZARELLA.

"Well?" we asked them. "What did you see?"

Ned took a deep BREATH.

"It was a g-ghost," he stammered. "A r-real g-ghost. He was standing in the middle of the arena, dressed like a GLADIATOR. He followed us around, waving a sword. He wanted to spear us like **MOUSE KEBABS**! Yikes!"

The tourists all quickly turned to leave.

"A ghost?!" one shouted. "No way! I'm not going in there."

"It's too **SCARY**!" another agreed.

The director tried to get them to change their minds.

"Come on," he squeaked desperately. "The Colosseum is so **inteResting**, and it's of **great historical value**."

But the tourists just shook their heads as they walked away. It was NO USE.

The director stood alone in front of the amphitheater, *tugging* at his whiskers.

"Alas, this is it!" he cried mournfully. "I'll be unemployed. Actually, I'm already **UNEMPLOYED**, because *nobody* wants to visit the Colosseum anymore!"

The ticket agent closed the ticket office.

"Boss, I won't come to work tomorrow," she said SADLY as she walked away, mumbling to herself. "I haven't sold a single **ticket** all week!"

Alas, this is it!

I won't be in tomorrow!

THE GLADIATOR GHOST

The director began to **SOB**.

Ratella tried to comfort him.

"Sir, please **don't worry**!" she said confidently. "Geronimo is going to go inside and prove that there's no GHOST because ghosts aren't real! Right, Stilton?"

Me?! *Why me?* But Ratella was already pushing me toward the entrance.

"Uh, I'll do my **best**," I squeaked nervously. "But shouldn't someone come with me?"

"Oh, no, you'll be fine," Ratella replied. "I'll just wait here with Benjamin and Trappy."

"Good luck, Uncle!" Benjamin squeaked.

I tried to *smile*, even though my teeth were chattering with fear. How could I let down my sweet little nephew?

"Be strong, Uncle G!" Trappy added.

So I walked toward the entrance, my **paws** trembling like warm baked Brie.

To calm myself, I kept repeating this mantra:

"Ghosts are not real . . . Ghosts are not real . . . Ghosts are not real . . ."

Go on, you'll be fine!

Ghosts are not real . . .

When I walked in, it was absolutely silent. I **admired** the circular arena in the center of the Colosseum and the old ruined **stands** all around me. Wow!

Reassured, I took a few steps, **repeating** to myself:

"Ghosts are not real . . . Ghosts are not real . . . Ghosts are not—"

Suddenly, an enormouse gladiator JUMPED

YOU WILL REGRET TAKING ON THE GLADIATOR GHOST!

How dare you enter the Colosseum?

in front of me, armed with a sword and a shield, just like an ancient **Roman**!

He took a step toward me and I took off as quickly as the **WIND**. You have no idea how fast I can run when I'm being **CHASED** by the ghost of a Roman gladiator!

He ran with long strides, the ground beneath him **shaking** with every pawstep he took. Somehow, I managed to outrun him!

Help!

I sprinted out of the Colosseum and COLLAPSED in a heap.

Ratella Spywhiskers, Benjamin, Trappy, and the director of the Colosseum surrounded me.

"Well?" Ratella asked hopefully.

"T-there really is a g-ghost!" I squeaked between breaths. "**HELP!**"

"I already know that, Geronimo!" Ratella replied with a huff. "Tell me **something** new!"

Then she knelt next to me and whispered into my left ear:

Calm down!

Well?

Uncle?

T-there really is a g-ghost . . .

"Agent **OOG**, I demand you go back inside the Colosseum immediately, and this time, I want **RESULTS**."

"W - what about the ghost?"

I stammered in reply.

"Do you think that two secret agents would have been assigned to this mission if it was going to be **EASY**, Geronimo? Find out who he is and why he's there!" she asked. "Remember, you can use ALL the tools inside the secret-agent suitcase. So get back in there **NOW**, understand?!"

I excused myself for a moment and left Ratella with Benjamin and Trappy. Then I went over to a BENCH opposite the Colosseum.

There, I **calmly** went through all the tools in my suitcase. I saw a *map* of Rome and a

plastic bag printed with these instructions:

Vacuum-packed Roman gladiator costume. Pull cord to open.

Cautiously, I pulled the **cord**. A second

A gladiator costume? Pull the cord?

later, out **popped** the perfect gladiator costume, complete with a shield and a helmet. (It had all been vacuum-packed!) I rushed to put **EVERYTHING** on.

The perfect gladiator costume!

Helmet

Shield

Armor

Protective sandals

Coconut Ice Cream

I realized there were **INSTRUCTIONS** on the back of the map:

To access the secret entrance to the Colosseum, you must go to the ice cream cart in front of the Colosseum. The vendor will point out the secret passageway. Just say the phrase: "Coconut ice cream with whipped cream, toasted almonds, and a cherry on top." Then stick out your tongue!

I saw an ICE CREAM CART right in front of me, so I followed the instructions. But instead of giving me ice cream and directions to a secret passageway, the vendor looked insulted.

"How *rude*!" he squeaked. "Why are you sticking out your tongue at me?"

I quickly realized there was **ANOTHER** ice cream

cart in front of the Colosseum. I scampered over there and ordered again. This time when I stuck out my tongue, the vendor **winked** back and handed me an ICE CREAM CONE. I licked it and discovered a note in the whipped cream:

Special Agent 00G: Take thirty steps to the right *toward the newsstand opposite the Colosseum.* Then take four steps to the left *toward the crooked tree.*

Take ten steps forward *toward the water fountain.* Turn around *and you will see a manhole cover.*

Special Agent OOG:
TAKE THIRTY STEPS TO THE RIGHT toward the newsstand opposite the Colosseum. Then take FOUR STEPS TO THE LEFT toward the crooked tree. TAKE TEN STEPS FORWARD toward the water fountain. TURN AROUND and you will see a manhole cover. Lift it and CLIMB IN CAREFULLY, but be sure to PIN YOUR SNOUT SHUT with the clothespin first.

Lift it and climb in carefully, *but be sure to* pin your snout shut *with the clothespin first.*

How strange! Why did I need to pin my snout shut with a clothespin? I had a feeling I was about to find out. So I **CAREFULLY** lifted the manhole cover and climbed in. As soon as it closed behind me, I understood why I was wearing a clothespin — even with it on, the **smell** was **OVERWHELMING**. I had just walked into a **sewer**!

What a stench!

A SECRET PASSAGEWAY

It was really **dark** down in the sewer! I put on my **night vision** goggles and walked carefully down a VERY NARROW sidewalk along a drain tunnel.

The tunnel was filled with foaming, **stinky**, **greenish** water. My whiskers trembled at the thought of falling in. Cheese and crackers, it was so **disgusting**!

Every so often, I heard a loud **buzz** and strange metallic sounds: **click, clack, click, clack**. I pulled out my secret-agent umbrella and turned it to flashlight mode.

Finally, I saw a fluorescent green sign on a wall that glowed in the dark. It read: **Special Agent OOG, climb this ladder!**

I cautiously scampered up the slippery steps,

being careful not to **LOOK** down. When I got to the top of the ladder, I found another **MANHOLE COVER**. I lifted it and climbed through to discover . . . a room full of **ENORMOUSE** spiders!

Moldy mozzarella! What were these spiders doing there? There were so

many of them, and they were **HUGE**! They scampered around while glaring menacingly at me with their **beady little eyes**.

I tried to run away, but I kept getting caught up in their **sticky** webs . . .

Somehow, I was able to **break free** from the webs. I scampered away as quickly as I could,

but the **BIGGEST** spider followed me!

"Help!" I cried. "I don't want to **lose my fur**!"

Ahead of me, I saw a small opening in the wall. **Desperately**, I tried to wiggle my body through it, but my tail got **CAUGHT**. Unfortunately, the spider took advantage of the opportunity and **pinched** me on the butt.

"Ouchie!" I squeaked.

I was able to **pull myself through** the opening. **GREAT GOUDA**, I was saved! But where was my secret-agent suitcase? Cracker crumbs, I had left it behind! What a **NIGHTMARE**!

I reached back through the opening with my **paw** and felt around for the suitcase, struggling to find it.

A second later . . . SQUEAK! I HAD IT!

INSIDE THE COLOSSEUM

Wow! What an adventure! I paused for a minute to catch my breath. When I turned around, I was in for another **shock**: Ratella Spywhiskers was standing right in front of me!

"**Yikes!**" I squeaked. "W-what are you doing here? I mean, **how did you get in?**"

"I came in through another **secret** passageway," she whispered. "I'm a secret agent, too, remember? I decided to come **HELP** you. I figured you would **NEVER** make it without me. I brought Benjamin and Trappy along, but I didn't tell them we're secret agents."

At that moment, two **familiar** little snouts popped up behind her: it was Benjamin and Trappy!

"Hi, *Uncle G*!" Benjamin said as he gave me a hug.

"We came to help you find the GHOST," Trappy squeaked. "Isn't that **GREAT**?"

"But it's too dangerous!" I replied, **worried**.

"Aw, please?" Benjamin said sweetly, a pleading look in his eyes. "It will be an **adventure**! I'm so glad I came to Rome with you. This is the greatest trip I've ever been on!

Hi, Uncle G!

Yikes!

"These **ancient** ruins are so cool. You were right, Uncle G — history is fun!"

Hearing those words reminded me that at least part of my mission in Rome had been a **SUCCESS**: history was really coming *alive* for my nephew!

"Of course you and Trappy can come along," I said, giving in. "But stay close to us, and be **careful**!"

I told them about the spiders I had encountered. Then we looked around and discovered that we were on the lower level of the Colosseum. I explained to Benjamin and Trappy that the shows held there were often **BRUTAL**: gladiators, who were usually slaves or criminals, were made to fight against other gladiators and against **wild animals**.

As we explored the passageways underneath the Colosseum, I noticed ancient objects were

GLADIATORS AND THE COLOSSEUM

The Roman Colosseum was commissioned by Roman Emperor Vespasian and took more than ten years to build. It was completed in 80 CE during the rule of Emperor Titus. The Colosseum held between 50,000 and 75,000 spectators. Emperors and other important Roman officials held public events in the Colosseum that included fights between gladiators or between gladiators and wild animals, as well as chariot races and theatrical plays. The Colosseum could also be filled with water to stage sea battles (called *naumachiae*) during which the gladiators fought one another while aboard small ships.

There were as many as fifteen different classes of gladiator. Each used different weapons and armor. These four were some of the most common:

MIRMILLONE
Wore a helmet with a fish symbol on it and carried a sword and shield.

THRACIAN
Wore a helmet with a wide brim that covered the face and head and fought using a curved sword called a *sica*.

RETIARIUS
Carried a trident, a dagger, and a weighted net and wore a large *manica*, or arm guard, that extended to the shoulder and left side of the chest.

SECUTOR
Carried a curved, rectangular shield and a sharp dagger and wore a helmet with two small eyeholes.

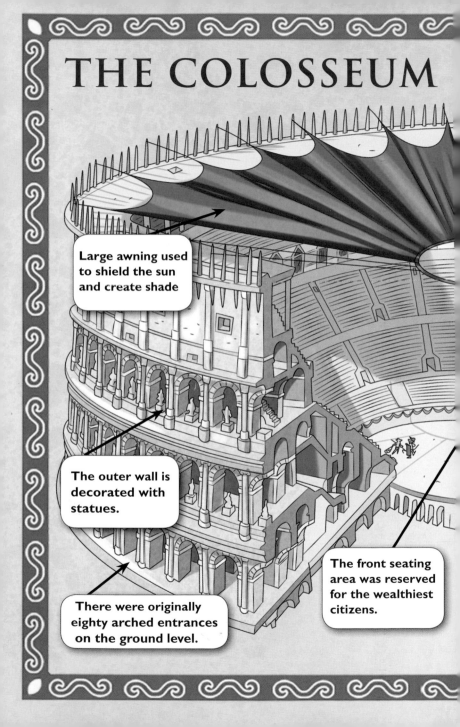

Awning supports

Public seating

Rooms and tunnels below the Colosseum held gladiators and wild animals.

Other passageways housed pulleys, elevators, and equipment.

everywhere. There were old-fashioned WOOD and brass chariots as well as weapons hanging on the walls. But, oddly, the items looked new rather than thousands of years old.

HOW STRANGE!

Suddenly, I heard voices SHOUTING. It sounded exactly like a live audience CHEERING before a gladiator fight.

What are all these ancient objects doing here?

What in the name of cheese was going on?

Could Ratella, Benjamin, Trappy, and I have gone *back in time* to the **EARLY DAYS** of the Colosseum? Had we somehow traveled not just to Rome, but to the time of the **GLADIATORS**, too?!

My Poor Whiskers!

A moment later, we heard a ROAR. We scampered up a ladder and ended up in front of one of the **entrances** to the arena. We quickly hid behind a thick wooden door. I opened it a crack and **peeked** inside the arena . . .

Holey cheese! What an incredible sight: the Colosseum's stone stands were filled with thousands of ancient Romans! There were farmers, merchants, priests, soldiers, and Romans of all ages waiting for the fights to begin.

Opposite us was the *Imperial Box*, which is where the emperor and his trusted advisors sat. The emperor lifted a paw and the whole crowd CHEERED. Then a gladiator emerged from a side door and walked toward the center of the arena.

It was the gladiator ghost!

We watched from behind the wooden door as he began to warm up by **SWINGING** his sword back and forth. He was **VERY, VERY** close to us!

It's the gladiator ghost!

Suddenly, the gladiator ghost waved his **sword** so violently it grazed my helmet and **SHEARED OFF** my whiskers!

"Help!" I squeaked before I could stop myself.

"My poor whiskers!"

"Holey cheese!" Ratella whispered. "How strange. If he sheared off your whiskers, he can't be a ghost. He's a real gladiator!"

Unfortunately for all of us, the gladiator heard my scream. He stopped warming up immediately and instead started CHASING me! As he gained on us, Ratella squeaked: "Quick, Stilton: use the suitcase!"

I frantically rummaged through the suitcase, trying to come up with a plan.

What could I use to stop a dangerous gladiator? Ah, the glue! I took out a small packet of SUPERGLUE and spread it on the ground in a sticky puddle. Luckily for me, the gladiator ghost got STUCK in it!

But he just slipped off his FOOTWEAR and ran after us again!

"Quick, Stilton!" Ratella squeaked again. "Use the suitcase!"

Of course!

I rummaged through it again, and this time I took out the **GRAY TABLET**. I tossed it to the ground, and a thick cloud of smoke formed, blocking us from the gladiator's view.

Argh!

As we ran through the Colosseum, the crowd **CHANTED** at the gladiator encouragingly: "Get them! Get them! Get them!"

There!

I turned toward the Imperial Box and pleaded with the emperor for **MERCY**. "Excuse me!" I squeaked. "Yoo-hoo, Mr. Emperor! We haven't done anything WRONG. Please tell that gladiator to stop chasing us!"

But at that moment, Ratella grabbed me by my ear and DRAGGED me away.

"If you really care for your fur, follow me!" she squeaked.

A Daring Escape

Benjamin, Trappy, and I followed Ratella all the way to the TOP LEVEL of the Colosseum. We had nowhere else to run. We couldn't go back DOWN because the gladiator ghost was sure to get us. But we couldn't go any farther UP because we were already at the top!

Trappy and Benjamin looked very worried.

"Uncle G, what are we going to do now?" Benjamin squeaked softly.

HOLEY CHEESE, we were trapped! WHAT COULD WE DO?

"We need a plan!" Ratella replied. "It looks like the gladiator ghost is determined to *get us*! And he's not the only one . . ."

"Look!" Benjamin shouted suddenly. "Over there!"

He pointed across the Colosseum and I gasped. **Holey cheese!** A bunch of **ROMAN SOLDIERS** were climbing up to the top of the Colosseum. They were heading right toward us!

"I have an idea!" Ratella squeaked. She **GRABBED** the secret-agent umbrella and pressed the special button that turned it into a **hot-air balloon**! We quickly climbed into the basket. Then we **slowly** floated down to the center of the arena, leaving the soldiers and the gladiator at the top of the Colosseum.

We were safe!

Wait a minute . . . No, we weren't!

I realized there was a lion in the center of the arena. First it was pacing back and forth. When it noticed us it came closer, **GROWLING** at us with its jaws wide open. I **BRAVELY** faced

the lion, standing between it and Trappy and Benjamin to protect them.

Twisted rattails! I didn't want to become lion food!

Luckily, I opened my umbrella and pressed the **emergency-shield** button just in time! Phew! SAVED BY A WHISKER!

Still, the lion had raised its paw and was about to **strike**. I prepared for the collision, covering

I'll protect you!

my snout with my paws, but . . .

NOTHING HAPPENED!

NOTHING HAPPENED!

NOTHING NOTHING NOTHING

NOTHING NOTHING

NOTHING NOTHING

NOTHING NOTHING

NOTHING

NOTHING

How Dare You, Stilton?

I peeked out from behind the umbrella shield. **What was going on?** Why hadn't the lion **pounced** on me? Then I realized something — the lion was just a **holographic** projection! It wasn't real!

I looked around and discovered many beams of **light** shining toward the center of the arena. The light was coming from huge projectors that had been hidden in the Colosseum's stands. None of it had been real . . . It was all an illusion!

I ran toward the stands, which were **crowded** with cheering citizens. But as I got closer, I bumped into a **GIANT** movie screen! **HOLEY CHEESE**, the entire Colosseum had been turned into a huge 3-D movie theater. Someone had even thought to add SPECIAL EFFECTS like bad smells so we would think we had traveled back in time!

I turned back toward the **CENTER** of the arena. There was the GLADIATOR GHOST! He had made his way down from the top of the Colosseum.

"I'm not AFRAID of you!" I squeaked boldly. "You're not even *real*!"

Huh?!

Then I ran straight toward him until . . .

Bonk!

Moldy mozzarella! I thought I could walk right through the projection of the gladiator, but I was **wrong**. The gladiator wasn't a hologram — it was a **ROBOT**!

Squeak! Ouch, that hurt!

I smashed into the robot so hard, it broke into pieces.

I'm not afraid of you!

"I am the Glad —" the robot **CROAKED** before it powered down completely and lay motionless on the ground like a mound of scrap metal.

Suddenly, there was a shout from the Imperial Box.

"How dare you, Stilton!"

BONK!

Ouch, that hurt!

I ran toward the image of the fake emperor, pulled the movie screen aside, and found myself in the middle of a secret room full of **massive supercomputers**!

It was NED and **EARL NOSYSNOUT**! And there was a *gigantic* screen above them displaying Madame No's scowling snout.

"You two are USELESS!" she squeaked at Ned and Earl. "You are one hundred percent incompetent!"

Then she turned her gaze on me.

"You may have **won** this round, Stilton, but this isn't over yet!"

The screen went **BLACK**. Outside the Colosseum, I heard an engine revving up, followed by the sound of squealing tires. I had a feeling it

was Madame No in her leopard-print limousine, making a quick getaway!

Ned and Earl glanced at each other in **alarm**. Then they, too, tried to run!

I quickly *popped* open the secret-agent suitcase and spread some **SUPERGLUE** on the ground. The glue created a sticky puddle that TRAPPED the two thugs.

They weren't going anywhere!

THE COLOSSEUM GHOST HOAX

Quick, come to the Colosseum!

I called the police and quickly explained what had happened. I had a feeling they would be very interested in talking to Ned and Earl Nosysnout.

But the director of the Colosseum was still very CONFUSED.

"I just don't understand," he squeaked as he stood there scratching his head. "How did that GLADIATOR GHOST appear in the Colosseum?"

"Well, I can't be sure, but I think I have an idea," I explained. "Madame No and the EGO

Corp had a **plan**: they wanted to make the Colosseum worthless so that they could buy it at a **very low** price. Then she could build a new real-estate development there!

"But Madame No didn't want anyone to know it was her. So she hired Ned and Earl Nosysnout to set everything up. They BUILT the control room and brought in the ROBOT. And since Ned Nosysnout is a famous reporter, he wrote about the ghost in the newspaper so that tourists would be too SCARED to visit the Colosseum anymore!

"Then Ned and Earl had to be sure everyone believed there really was a ghost. So they screened a *sophisticated* 3-D movie all around the arena's seating area. That way anyone standing in the middle of the arena would be CONVINCED that it was all **real**! Ned and Earl even added special effects, like **stinky** sewer smells! The gladiator ghost was actually one of Madame No's **ROBOTS**, not a holographic projection."

The director nodded his head. A small crowd had gathered around him as well, and they were all shocked at the incredible tale I had just told.

"So, in other words," I concluded dramatically, "none of this is **REAL**!"

Ratella raised her eyebrows at me. Then she leaned over to whisper in my ear.

"Agent 00G, you do realize this means the enormouse spiders you ran into in the sewer were **FAKE**, too, right?"

"Of course!" I squeaked, my fur turning **red** with embarrassment. "I mean, everyone knows enormouse sewer spiders aren't a **REAL** thing! They just looked so **SCARY**, I couldn't help being frightened!"

At that moment, police officers escorted Ned and Earl Nosysnout right past me. They looked FURIOUS.

"Stilton, why did you have to stick your whiskers where they didn't belong?" Ned squeaked.

"Yeah!" Earl added. "You should have minded your own business!"

"That would have been impossible," I squeaked right back. "Whenever there's a MYSTERY to be solved, an injustice to correct, or news to be shared, well, then readers of *The Rodent's Gazette* have a right to know! And that's my job, or my name isn't Stilton, *Geronimo Stilton*!"

None of this is real!

Then I called the **newspaper**.

"Hello? It's Geronimo," I said. "I have an **exclusive** story from Rome. The headline should read: 'The Hunt for the Colosseum Ghost'!"

Then I went through the details of what had happened. The following day, my grandfather William called me. For once, he had something **nice** to say!

Hi, Grandfather!

"**Congratulations**, Grandson!" he squeaked. "Well done! Your article on the Colosseum ghost has helped us sell more copies than any other paper in town. Sally Ratmousen at *The Daily Rat* is very, very jealous! **Ha, ha, ha!**"

Sally is my fiercest **rival**, and *The Daily Rat* is *The Rodent's*

Gazette's biggest competitor.

"Good for you, Grandson," my grandfather continued. "I'm proud of you! And I'm sorry I scolded you for **traveling** to Italy.

"I understand now that you need to travel to get **new ideas** and to have access to exclusive stories. In other words, *you were right*."

I could barely believe my ears. Grandfather

Congratulations, Grandson!

didn't often admit to being **wrong**!

"By the way," he continued. "I know I don't tell you often enough, but remember that I love you."

I smiled.

"Thank you, Grandfather!" I squeaked. "I love you, too!"

I hung up the phone and hugged Benjamin and Trappy.

"I love you both so much!" I told them. "Sometimes we forget to say that to the ones closest to us!"

Benjamin hugged me back.

"Thanks, Uncle!" he squeaked. "When I grow up, I want to be a fearless reporter just like you!"

Trappy **winked** at me.

"Well, to be honest, I think sometimes Uncle G gets **SCARED**," she said. "But he is brave. I love you, too, Uncle!"

"Congratulations, Agent 00G," Ratella said quietly. "MISSION ACCOMPLISHED!"

GOOD-BYE, ITALY!

It was time for us to leave Rome and return to New Mouse City. As we boarded our flight home, I composed this poem:

Oh, Rome, what a fair city,
Full of ruins and ancient history!
Statues, fountains, pizza, and more,
We'll soon be back for another tour!

Ah, Italy!

My home was in New Mouse City, but I was sad to leave such a **special** place.

You'll never guess who came to meet me when I got off

the plane—**CREEPELLA**! She brought her entire family with her in her **TURBORAPID 3000**!

She ran up to me and hugged me **tightly**.

"My little Gerryberry, do you know what day it is?" she squeaked sweetly. "It's the anniversary of our first date! You didn't forget, did you?"

"Creepella," I said kindly. "I'm so **happy** to see you! But you do know that we aren't dating, right? We're just **good friends**!"

Hi, Gerryberry!

"What?" her father, Boris, squeaked. "You're not her boyfriend? Why not? It's very clear to me you two are *made for each other*!"

"Even though there won't be an anniversary party tonight, we can still *celebrate* something important — OUR FRIENDSHIP!" I replied. "Creepella, you and your family are my friends, and I love you all dearly. Please come to my house and I'll make a **very special** pizza for us to share!"

"Pizza?!" the von Cacklefur family replied. "We love pizza!"

The friendship party was fabumouse!

The next day, Benjamin went to school and had a QUIZ on ancient Rome. Thanks to his firsthand experience on our trip, he aced the test! He came home waving his paper proudly.

"I did it, Uncle G!" he squeaked happily. "LOOK!"

SECRET-AGENT COOKBOOK

THREE-VEGETABLE PIZZA

BE SURE TO ASK AN ADULT FOR HELP!

INGREDIENTS:

- ½ cup sliced zucchini
- ½ cup sliced eggplant
- chopped thyme and rosemary
- ½ cup cherry tomatoes
- extra-virgin olive oil
- salt
- 1 pound pizza dough
- flour
- 1 cup shredded mozzarella

DIRECTIONS:

Preheat the oven to 500°F. Grill the zucchini and eggplant for a few minutes, then put on a plate and set aside. Sprinkle with thyme and rosemary. Cut the cherry tomatoes in halves, then drizzle with olive oil and a touch of salt. Line two cookie sheets with parchment paper. Divide the dough in half. Roll out each piece into a circle on a floured surface, then lay it on the parchment paper. Sprinkle the dough with the mozzarella, followed by the grilled vegetables. Drizzle with olive oil and sprinkle lightly with salt. Bake for twenty minutes. As soon as you remove the pizza from the oven, add the tomatoes and serve immediately.

I realized that Principal Strictfur had helped me when I had been a student, and I had helped Benjamin in the same way. Maybe one day Benjamin will help someone else develop a *love* of history, too!

I thought for a moment about how satisfying it is to share with those we love, whether it's a special PIZZA or a love of knowledge. The warm feeling I get inside from helping others is even better than a slice of Mouse Island's finest cheese!

And now, my dear readers, I'm afraid this story must come to an **end**. Farewell until the next adventure!

Look, Uncle!

Now check out this bonus
Mini Mystery story!
Join me in solving a whisker-licking-
good mystery. Find clues along with me
as you read. Together, we'll be
super-squeaky investigators!

THE CHEESE BURGLAR

A GARBAGE CAN FOR MR. STILTON!

It was a beautiful Saturday morning in spring. I was dusting the display case that held my precious cheese rind collection. You see, I have rinds dating from all the way back to the sixth century! They are my most prized possessions.

Oh, I'm so sorry, I almost forgot to introduce myself. My name is Stilton, Geronimo Stilton, and I run *The Rodent's Gazette*, the most famouse newspaper on Mouse Island.

So, I was dusting my display case when the doorbell **rang**. I opened the door to find a yellow garbage can with a sign that read: SECURITY SYSTEM.

HOW STRANGE! I hadn't ordered a security system.

Before I could squeak a word, the garbage can started rolling toward me and followed me right inside.

HOW WEIRD!

I closed the door and followed the garbage can into the living room. It just kept going! This was **VERY PECULIAR**. The garbage can started rolling around. It knocked over a couple of chairs and a **china** vase. Then it slid toward my precious cheese rind display case!

I sprang *FORWARD* and tried to stop it. As soon as my paw touched the lid, a siren blared.

Moldy mozzarella! I had accidentally set off the alarm! I tried desperately to turn it off.

Suddenly, the garbage can spit out a sheet of paper. **"To deactivate the alarm, insert two (or three) bananas!"**

I finally understood.

"**NOT AGAIN!**" I shouted. "Get your tail out of there right now!"

The garbage can's lid lifted up, and a snout I knew well peeked out.

"**Hello, my dear Stilton!** How did you like my little prank?"

THE M.I.C.E. CONVENTION

It was my old friend Hercule Poirat, the detective! Hercule and I have been **friends** since we were just wee mouselets. I love him dearly, but I've always hated his pranks.

"Why in the name of cheese would you **DO** something like this?" I asked.

"Well, today you're going to present your cheese rind collection at **M.I.C.E.**, the annual Mouse Island Cheese Exhibition. So I thought that you might need a security system. The infamouse **Cheese Rind Bandit** is supposed to be there!"

"Rancid rat hairs!" I exclaimed. I had forgotten all about **M.I.C.E.**! When I received the invitation, I wasn't sure whether or not I should go. But then I learned that 𝕻𝖗𝖔𝖋𝖊𝖘𝖘𝖔𝖗 𝕽𝖊𝖌𝖎𝖓𝖆𝖑𝖉 𝕽𝖎𝖓𝖉𝖗𝖆𝖙, the most famous cheese rind collector of all time, would be there. I **immediately** decided to attend.

The convention's **organizers** had offered each collector an **ARMORED CAR**

You are invited to participate
in the annual
MOUSE ISLAND CHEESE EXHIBITION
New Mouse City Exhibition Hall
Please R.S.V.P.

so we could transport our antique rinds safely and securely. I had agreed, because I, too, had heard that the Cheese Rind Bandit was planning on making an appearance.

I looked at my watch: **IT WAS 9:50!**

"The armored car will be here in ten minutes," I exclaimed. "I have to hurry!"

"Do you need help, my dear Stilton?" asked Hercule.

"No, thank you."

"I can hold open your

suitcase if you want me to."

"No, thank you!"

"Would you like a banana?"

"No, thank you!!"

"Here, let me peel one for you."

"No, thank youuuuuuuu!!!"

At that moment, the doorbell rang.

"Stilton, the armored car is here! Why don't I open the door for you?"

"Oh, all right, fine! open the door!"

TWO HELPERS, PLUS ONE MORE

Fortunately, it was not the armored car. It was my nephew **BENJAMIN** and his friend Bugsy Wugsy. They scurried in the front door.

"Hi, Uncle Geronimo!" Benjamin exclaimed. "Everything ready for the convention?"

"Hi, Benjamin," I said. I just adore that little mouse. "Yes, I'm almost ready."

"Hello, Mr. Poirat!" Bugsy Wugsy said. "Are you exhibiting at the convention, too?"

"Not really," replied Poirat, peeling a banana. "My dear friend Stilton needed a helping paw, since he is clumsier than a gopher in a garbage can. So here I am!"

"Hmpf!" I muttered under my breath. "I'm not *that* clumsy!"

At that exact moment, I slipped on

the banana peel Poirat had dropped on the floor. **CRUSTY CHEESE RINDS**, what a tumble!

"Are you hurt, Uncle G?" Bugsy Wugsy asked.

She moved forward and accidentally **STEPPED** on my tail. *Yee-ouch!*

"Uncle, do you need our **help**,

too?" Benjamin asked sweetly.

"We'll help you display your cheese **rinds**!" Bugsy Wugsy offered.

"Well, I don't know . . ." I began.

"We'll keep an eye out for SUSPICIOUS rodents!"

"Well, I don't know . . ."

"Don't damage your little gray cells, Stilton," Poirat said. "Let us help!"

"Oh, all right!" I finally agreed. I didn't seem to have a choice! "You can all come to the convention with me."

Just then, we heard the sound of a car horn out on the street.

Beep! Beep!

ARE YOU MR. STILTON?

Bugsy Wugsy peeked out the window. "There's a **VAN** here, with a driver all dressed in **black**. She's waiting for you, Uncle G."

I opened the door. On the stoop stood a rodent with dark glasses and curly blond fur.

"Are you Mr. Stilton?" she asked.

"Yes, that's me," I replied.

"I'm doing security for **M.I.C.E.**," she explained. "I'm here to escort you to the exhibition hall."

"Oh yes, I'm **ready**!" I replied without thinking.

"Really?" She looked me over from snout to tail. "Because it looks like you're still in your **pajamas**."

"Oh yes, er, of course I am," I mumbled nervously. "Just give me one minute, please."

It took me:

TEN seconds to wash my face.

TEN seconds to brush my teeth.

TEN seconds to get dressed.

FIVE seconds to comb my fur.

TWENTY seconds to stow the cheese rinds in my steel briefcase.

FIVE seconds to lock the door.

I was ready in exactly one minute! The security rodent was incredibly impressed.

A DANGEROUS DRIVER

I shook the security rodent's **paw**.

"My name is Ashley Dow," she said. "But you can call me Ash. Climb in and hold on tight!"

I scrambled into the van. Ash's powerful **perfume** made my snout spin. Hercule, Benjamin, and Bugsy Wugsy climbed in, too. The van sprang away from the curb faster than a **mousetrap spring**. **Jumping gerbil babies!** I was terrified.

"Stilton," Hercule hissed. He was as **PALE** as a slice of mozzarella. "Can you ask your new friend to slow down?"

"Yes, Uncle Geronimo," Benjamin agreed. "I'm feeling sick." His snout was as **green** as moldy cheddar.

But Bugsy Wugsy seemed fine. "Wow, this is like a **roller coaster**!" she exclaimed. "You're a great driver, Ms. Dow!"

"Thanks!" Ash replied. "You're **sweeter** than cheddar cheesecake."

Ash stopped the car in front of the exhibition hall.

"**Here we are**," she said.

As we scurried out of the van, I noticed something dangling from the wrist of Ash's uniform.

CLUE 1

What did Geronimo notice?

13

UNLUCKY NUMBER THIRTEEN

Ash, Hercule, Benjamin, Bugsy Wugsy, and I scampered into the **ENORMOUSE** exhibition hall.

We followed Ash through the booths, where collectors from every part of Mouse Island were showing off their precious cheese rinds. There were rinds from every era, from **prehistory** to the period of the Great

Cat War, all the way to the Battle of Rateloo.

Ash stopped in front of BOOTH 13.

"Here's your booth, Mr. Stilton," she said. "I hope you're not superstitious. **Good luck!**"

With that, she left with a shake of her long blond fur.

Hercule pulled out a banana and started **nibbling**. "Move those paws, Stilton," he said. "Booth number **THIRTEEN** is unlucky! We should try to switch with someone."

"I don't believe in bad luck," I began. Actually, I did, but I didn't want to say so in front of Benjamin.

Before I could continue, I slipped on the banana peel Hercule had just dropped on the floor.

"See, Stilton?" Hercule said as he, Benjamin, and Bugsy Wugsy reached down to **HELP** me get up. "I was right. Today seems to be your *unlucky* day!"

A UNIQUE RIND

"Are you **HURT**, Mr. Stilton?" came a squeak from behind me.

I whirled around and immediately recognized the rodent standing there. "**Reginald Rindrat**, Mouse Island's most famous cheese rind collector!" I squeaked.

"Yes, that's me," he replied. "And it is a great HONOR to have you as a neighbor, Mr. Stilton. My booth is right here, number **fourteen**!"

"How nice of you to introduce yourself," Hercule **interrupted**. "I am Hercule Poirat, world-renowned private investigator and Geronimo Stilton's best friend. I am here to guard his **VERY PRECIOUS** cheese rind collection."

"I've heard a lot about your magnificent **COLLECTION**," replied

Rindrat, shaking my paw. "Please come with me. I want to show you something truly **UNIQUE**!"

Reginald Rindrat led us to a small display case. He removed the cloth that covered it and switched on a light, revealing a cheese rind with a greenish **glow**.

"Why, this is the last surviving cheese **rind** from the world-famous Samuel Stinktail collection, dating back to the **sixteenth century**!" I exclaimed.

"That is correct, Mr. Stilton!" Rindrat

replied. "You are a true cheese connoisseur."

Samuel Stinktail

"I've been hunting for this cheese rind since I was just a mouselet," I **confessed**. "How did you find it?"

"That is my little **secret**!" Rindrat replied with a chuckle.

Hercule examined the display case. "This glass is so fragile . . . isn't that a little dangerous?"

"**DANGEROUS?** Not a chance!" replied a squeak from behind us. "Our security systems are the safest in the world."

A SUPER SECURITY SYSTEM

I turned to find myself snout-to-snout with an elegant female rodent just as Hercule stepped on my paw.

OUCH, OUCH, OUCHIE!

The lovely rodent had long blond **fur** and wore dark glasses.

Ouchie!

"My name is Flora Ratson," she said. "I'm the convention's director."

"Nice to meet you," I squeaked. "My name is Geronimo Stil—"

"Mr. Stilton, of course!" she exclaimed. "We've been waiting for you. You and Professor Rindrat are our guests of honor. Because your antique cheese rinds are so valuable, we are providing  you with our state-of-the-art, super-high-tech security system."

She stepped toward Rindrat's display case and attached a special KEYPAD.

"It's very easy to use," she explained.

"Just follow these **simple** steps:

1. Pick a five-number combination.

2. Memorize the combination.

3. Press each key once.

"If you tap the wrong key, the **alarm** will immediately go off."

"What if someone figures out the combination?" Benjamin asked.

"The keypad is programmed to recognize only your unique **PAWPRINT**," Ms. Ratson explained. "If another rodent tries to press the same keys, the alarm will go off."

"**How fabumouse!**" Rindrat exclaimed.

"Just let me clean the keys and you can choose your combination." Ms. Ratson said. "If there are traces of other pawprints, the system won't work properly."

She **sprayed** the keypad, and then asked us to turn around while Professor Rindrat chose his **five** numbers.

After Rindrat was done, we moved to my booth. Ms. Ratson used the **spray** and I selected my combination.

When I'd finished, Ms. Ratson said good-bye and scurried off.

BENJAMIN and Bugsy Wugsy exchanged a strange look.

"What's up?" I asked them.

"Would you clean a keypad like that, Uncle G?" Bugsy Wugsy asked.

"And would you wear **sunglasses** inside?" Benjamin asked.

I shrugged. "I don't know . . . Maybe I would if I were like Ms. Ratson. She's as cool as iced cheese!"

CLUE 2

Bugsy Wugsy and Benjamin seem suspicious of Ms. Ratson. Why?

A LITTLE
ACCIDENT

"I agree, my dear Stilton!" said Hercule.
"I think that rodent is a big **LIAR**!"

"But she's the **DIRECTOR** of the
convention," I protested.

"That may be true, but I'd still like to
take a little look around this place," he
replied before he
disappeared.

Meanwhile,
Benjamin and
Bugsy Wugsy
helped me create
an **attractive**

display of cheese rinds inside my case. Then I carefully entered my combination on the KEYPAD.

"Now that the rinds are safe, let's go take a look **around**!" I told Benjamin and Bugsy Wugsy.

The show was marvemouse. There were dozens of rare rinds, including one extremely rare prehistoric cheese fOSSiL.

As we were walking by Professor Rindrat's booth, I stopped to admire Stinktail's rind.

All of a sudden, a rodent burst out

from behind a display case.

"**YOOOOO-hoooo!** I've made an interesting discovery!"

It was Hercule Poirat, of course!

"Why are you wearing those YELLOW gloves?" I asked my friend.

"Well, my dear Stilton," he replied, "I spotted the director wearing gloves just like these! She secretly pressed the keypad and . . . guess what? The alarm did not go off! Look."

He stretched his paw toward Rindrat's display case.

"**NOOOOOOOO!**" I cried. I tried to stop him, but I stumbled, and my paw

landed right on the keypad. The alarm went off with a deafening screech.

WHEEE-OOOOO-WHEEE-OOOOO-WHEEE-OOOOO!

Security agents surrounded me instantly. And they were all pointing at me as if I were a **THIEF**!

Flora Ratson immediately scurried to the scene. "Please, gentlemice,

everything is okay," she told the agents. "It was an **accident**."

Then she turned to me. "See, Mr. Stilton? No chance of theft! Let me clean the keypad." As she **sprayed** the keys again, I noticed she was indeed wearing black **GLOVES**.

"Uncle G, did you see that?" Bugsy Wugsy asked.

CLUE 3

What did Bugsy Wugsy see?

STICKY PAWS

Before I could reply, **Professor Rindrat** scampered toward me. "Mr. Stilton, I am very sorry about what just happened."

"Oh, **thank you**!" I replied. "I thought you would suspect me, too."

"Never!" he declared. "Not a **gentlemouse** like you! As a matter of fact, why don't we get a bite together?"

"What a nice idea!" I replied. Then I decided to really impress the professor. "I accept, but **only** if it's on me."

"That's very **kind** of you," Professor Rindrat said.

At that moment, Hercule's snout POKED OUT from behind a column. "Food? I'll join you!"

Right outside the exhibition hall there was a little restaurant with a strange name: THE BIG SPENDER BISTRO.

We were about to sit down when Rindrat excused himself.

"I must go wash my **PAWS**," he said. "They feel STICKY."

"Me too," I replied, following him.

When we returned to the table, Poirat was already ordering.

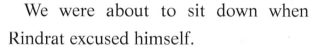

"Yes, I'd like to start with **one** appetizer of mixed bananas, **two** servings of banana fondue, **three** banana omelets, **four** slices of banana bread, and **five** pieces of banana pie."

"Your friend has an exceptionally large **appetite**!" Professor Rindrat observed.

Bugsy Wusgy and Benjamin laughed.

Meanwhile, I was sweatier than a slimy slice of Swiss. I had taken a look at the prices on the menu. Now I knew why this place was called THE BiG SPENDER BiSTRO: to eat here, you had to be a **big spender**!

When the bill came, the meal cost more than my most **precious** antique cheese rind! But everybody seemed satisfied and full, and that made me **happy**.

We headed back to the hall so we wouldn't miss the opening speech of the

M.I.C.E. convention.

As we scampered along, I overheard a conversation between two passing rodents. "My right paw feels STICKY."

"Mine, too!" came the reply.

Hmm, that was interesting . . .

Benjamin noticed my thoughtful expression. "I think I know what's making everyone's paws sticky, Uncle Geronimo."

CLUE 4

What have all the M.I.C.E. attendees touched with their right paws?

IS IT SHE, OR NOT SHE?

Bugsy Wugsy, Benjamin, and I joined the rest of the rodents in the exhibition hall.

As for Hercule, he had **disappeared** again.

Annual Mouse Island Cheese Exhibition

All the major scholars of **Comparative Rindology** sat at a long table at the front of the hall.

I recognized Professor Ratoloff, author of the influential book **Rindology: Cheese Rinds from Prehistory to the Present**, and also Professor Scrimprat, whose manual **Rindonomics: 1,001 Fun Ways to Preserve Your Cheese Rind Collection** was one of my favorite books on collecting.

At last, Ms. Ratson scurried up to the

MICROPHONE. "Hello, cheese lovers! It is with great pleasure that we kick off our annual convention . . ."

Hercule had slipped into the seat behind me. "No! It can't be the same rodent!" he whispered.

"**Shhh!**" I said. "I can't hear a word she's squeaking!"

"But this rodent doesn't resemble her . . ." he continued.

"Shhh! Please, shut your snout!"

"Take my binoculars, Stilton!" Hercule insisted. "Does it look like her?"

"Like who?" I asked. "What are you squeaking about?"

"Actually, Uncle, I think Mr. Poirat is **RIGHT**," Benjamin whispered. "That mouse isn't the same rodent we **met** this morning!"

CLUE 5

How is this Flora Ratson different?

CLAPPING AND NAPPING

But if the rodent squeaking was the real Flora Ratson, then who had we met earlier?

?? **Who?**??

I turned around to tell Poirat he was right, but he had disappeared again!

Meanwhile, the director was finishing up her speech.

There was a round of **applause**.

Clap! Clap! Clap!

"And a hearty thank-you to our security guards," Ms. Ratson continued, gesturing to the agents lined up next to her on the stage.

There was a second round of **APPLAUSE**.

Clap! Clap! Clap!

I noticed Ash Dow was among the agents onstage.

"And a final thank-you goes to the

Annual Mouse

ASH DOW COMPANY for donating all our security systems!"

There was a third round of **aPPlause**!

Clap! Clap! Clap!

"And now, I turn the floor over to Professor Harry Snoozemouse, twelfth-century cheddar rind expert."

There was absolutely no **aPPlause**!

Within two minutes, every mouse was sound asleep, including me.

Zzzzz...

All of a sudden, Hercule **POKED** me.

"Wake up, Stilton!"

he squeaked. "Something is about to happen, I can tell. **JUST LOOK AT THE STAGE!**"

I looked at the stage. Poirat was right! In fact, something had already happened.

CLUE 6

What happened onstage?

STILTON IS A THIEF!

I had to admit Poirat's suspicions were right on the snout. Ash Dow was sneaking away!

Weird!

Poirat quickly FOLLOWED Ash.

I jumped up to FOLLOW Poirat.

Benjamin and Bugsy Wugsy jumped up to follow me.

Professor Kindrat noticed we were on the move. He jumped up to FOLLOW Benjamin and Bugsy Wugsy.

A moment later, Poirat lost Ash Dow . . . and we lost him!

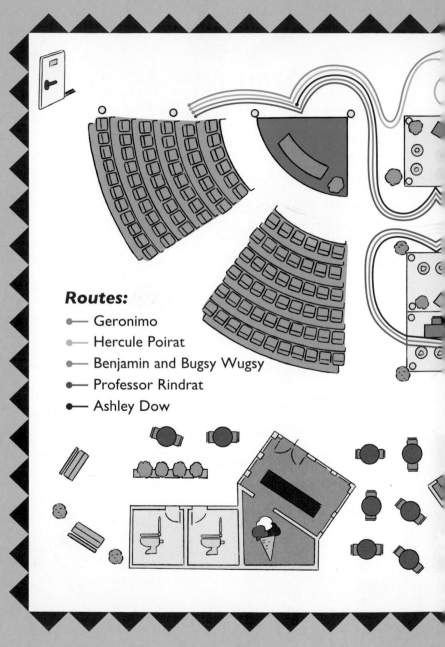

Routes:

- Geronimo
- Hercule Poirat
- Benjamin and Bugsy Wugsy
- Professor Rindrat
- Ashley Dow

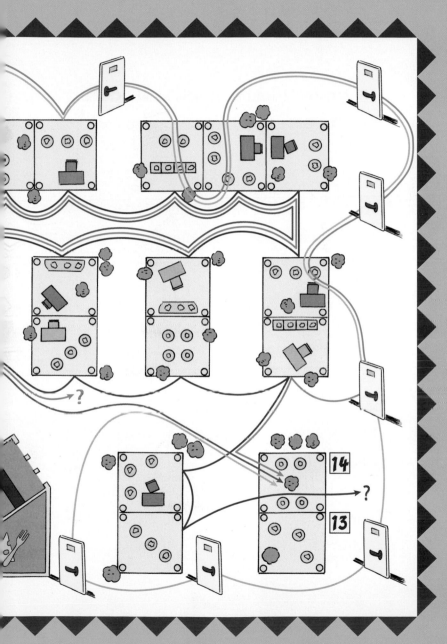

Somehow I found myself at **booth fourteen** — Professor Rindrat's booth.

All it took was a quick  around to realize what had happened. The display case containing Samuel Stinktail's rind was . . .

EMPTY!

Poirat scurried toward me.

"Stop, you cheddar-faced **THIEF**!" he yelled. Then he realized it was me. "Stilton? Don't tell me you've taken up **stealing**!"

At that moment, Professor Rindrat appeared behind him. When he saw

me next to the empty display case, he started **SHOUTING**, too.

"So it was no accident that you set off my alarm this morning!" Professor Rindrat squeaked. "You stole my precious rind! You are a thief, Stilton!"

CAUGHT IN
A TRAP

Security agents and nosy rind collectors **surrounded** me instantly.

Flora Ratson started to INTERROGATE me. "Mr. Stilton, confess! Where did you **hide** Mr. Rindrat's precious rind? And how did you avoid setting off the **alarm**?"

"It — it wasn't me," I stutTeREd. "I was following my friend Hercule Poirat, who was following the real **THIEF**."

Hercule stroked his whiskers thoughtfully. "Perhaps the real thief is playing **dirty** tricks on us. He's making Geronimo look **GUILTY** so we don't suspect him . . . or her!"

The other collectors scurried back to their booths to check on their own rinds. They had all disappeared!

Only **booth thirteen** (mine!) had not been robbed . . . How weird!

"It's Stilton!" someone shouted. "He's the **THIEF**!"

"Give us back our rinds, you rat burglar!"

"That's enough," Ms. Ratson snapped. "It's time to call the police!"

Crusty cheese rinds! I was being falsely accused! And I had no way to prove my innocence. I was trapped like a rat in a maze. I was going to JAIL for sure!

BLACK GLOVES AND SUNGLASSES

All of a sudden, I recognized a familiar squeak.

"**STOP, EVERYBODY!** It's not what you think."

"That's right!" another little squeak exclaimed. "Uncle G is not a thief!"

We have proof!

"Benjamin! Bugsy Wugsy!" I cried, hugging them. "Where have you been?"

"We FOLLOWED the thief, Uncle Geronimo!" Benjamin explained.

"Wait a minute, who are these mouselets?" Flora Ratson interrupted.

"My nephew and his friend," I said proudly. "And I'm sure they'll prove my **innocence**."

"Let's hear it, then," Ms. Ratson replied. "This better be good, or you're in **hot fondue**, Stilton!"

Benjamin started to explain. "This morning, a female rodent introduced herself to us with a **bogus** name. She said she was Flora Ratson. She gave us a **security system** for Uncle Geronimo's display case, and she told us how to set the alarm."

"What?" Flora Ratson **objected**. "I did no such thing!"

Bugsy Wugsy continued. "Right away, Benjamin and I wondered why she used **spray** on the system's keypad, and why she wore dark **sunglasses**,

The bogus director gave us a security system . . .

. . . and she sprayed something on the keys.

even inside the convention hall."

"I wondered about that, too," one of the collectors exclaimed.

"During the chase, the thief dropped her **glasses**!" Benjamin exclaimed. "Here, Ms. Ratson — try them on, and then look at the keypad."

"Holey cheese!" Flora Ratson squeaked. "With these on, I can tell

which **FIVE KEYS** Professor Rindrat has pressed!"

Bugsy Wugsy nodded. "And you can tell the order, too! The first one is the **darkest**, and then they get **lighter** as you get closer to the end of the combination!"

"So the spray was used to record the **pawprints**, not erase them!" a collector with brown fur said.

"That's why my paw was STICKY!" an elegant rodent added.

"But that imposter said the keypad would record our unique pawprints," another collector said.

"That's just one of many **LIES** she told," Benjamin replied. "Once a combination had been chosen, she used **BLACK GLOVES** to

avoid leaving her own pawprints. Here they are!"

"See, what did I tell you, Stilton?" Hercule interrupted. He showed me his **YELLOW GLOVES**. "I had already

figured out that part of her trick!"

THE HUNT FOR A THIEF

As more and more facts were uncovered, I felt myself relax like mozzarella MELTING in the sun. Benjamin and Bugsy Wugsy had saved my fur, **big time**!

"It looks like we owe you an apology, Mr. Stilton," Flora Ratson said. "We suspected you unfairly."

I blushed.

"Oh, please, it's

NOTHING," I mumbled.

"Now I understand why the **ASH DOW COMPANY** provided us with their security systems for *FREE*," Ms. Ratson went on. "It was all a trick!"

Benjamin, Bugsy Wugsy, and I looked at one another. The name of the company reminded us of something . . . but what?

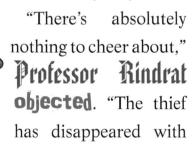

"**Yay!**" someone shouted. "We've solved the mystery!"

"There's absolutely nothing to cheer about," Professor Rindrat objected. "The thief has disappeared with

all our precious cheese rinds! "My
priceless Stinktail rind is
lost forever!"

"Blistering bananas!"
Poirat exclaimed. "I can't
believe what I'm hearing.
Okay, scrape the cheese out of your ears,
because I'm only going to say this once!
The crook cannot have **escaped**!"

"How can you be so sure about
that?" the professor asked him.

"Because my name is Hercule Poirat
and I am a great DETECTIVE,
isn't that right, my dear Stilton?"

Before I could reply, he went on.

"While I was pretending to FOLLOW

Ash Dow, I **LOCKED** this place up tighter than Ratlay's Bank. Our sly thief cannot have gone far!"

"By cheese, I think I've got it, Uncle Geronimo!" Benjamin exclaimed suddenly. "**ASH DOW** is an anagram for . . ."

CLUE 7

Rearrange the letters in Ash Dow. What do you get?

THE SHADOW!

But of course! **ASH DOW** was an anagram for **Shadow**!

The Shadow is an elusive thief who has made my snout spin on many other occasions!

And squeaking of my snout, at that moment something landed right on it! **"OUCH!"**

Busgy Wugsy picked it up. It was a black **BUTTON** with a white ZERO in the middle.

"Look!" Benjamin cried. "Up there!"

We all looked up. A blond rodent was climbing the rafters of the exhibition hall. And there was a big open window in the building's ceiling.

"She's getting away!" Ms. Ratson shouted.

The Shadow smirked, and kept on climbing. We could hear the sound of a helicopter outside.

Then we heard Poirat's squeak.

"Don't mess with Hercule Poirat!"

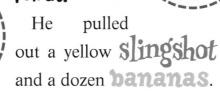

He pulled out a yellow slingshot and a dozen bananas.

"**WATCH OUT**, you sneaky thief!"

He aimed his slingshot.

The Shadow was just about to grab a ROPE and jump onto the helicopter when

she **slipped** on a banana peel. The bag she was carrying slid from her paws.

"Be careful, Ms. Shadow!" I shouted **nervously**. Even though she was a thief, I didn't want her to fall and break a paw.

But the Shadow had already grabbed the rope and was **swinging** onboard the chopper.

"**Burned banana bread!**" Poirat exclaimed, grabbing the bag as it fell toward us. He ripped it open. All the stolen rinds were inside!

By now the Shadow was safely on the helicopter. She wrinkled her snout at us and then blew me a **kiss**.

What a sly and slippery rodent!

THE SECOND RIND

The Shadow had **escaped**, but at least we all got our cheese rinds back.

I **invited** everyone over to celebrate.

The only rodent who couldn't make it was Hercule.

He said he had an *important*

appointment he simply could not miss.

After dessert, Professor Rindrat gave me a little **WOODEN BOX**. "Please accept this small gift as an apology. I shouldn't have accused you, Mr. Stilton."

I couldn't believe my **EYES**! "But this is . . . is . . ." I stuttered.

"One of Samuel Stinktail's cheese rinds," Rindrat finished. "I never told anybody there were **two**. I wanted to be the only rodent to own his rinds, but now I know there's another mouse **WORTHY** of collecting them!"

My whiskers were shaking with emotion. "How can I ever thank you?!"

Professor Rindrat smiled. "By putting that precious rind in a **safe** place!"

I nodded and scurried over to my display case. Then I turned PALER than a slice of mozzarella. "My cheese rinds have been **STOLEN**!" I cried.

At that moment, a yellow garbage can rolled into the room.

"To get your rinds back, insert two bananas," a sign on the can read. "Er, better make it three!"

"Hercule Poirat!" I exclaimed. "You get out of there this minute!"

The lid lifted up, and Hercule's *smirking* snout appeared.

"Oh, hello, my dear Stilton! Did you like my little prank?"

I couldn't help laughing. Hercule is a terrible prankster, but he's also a really **good** friend!

YOU'RE THE INVESTIGATOR!

DID YOU FIGURE OUT THE CLUES?

1 **What did Geronimo notice?**
There is a button dangling from the wrist of Ash's shirt.

2 **Bugsy Wugsy and Benjamin seem suspicious of Ms. Ratson. Why?**
Flora is wearing her sunglasses for no reason, and she sprayed the keypad without drying the keys.

3 **What did Bugsy Wugsy see?**
There is a button dangling from the wrist of Flora Ratson's shirt!

4 **What have all the M.I.C.E. attendees touched with their right paws?**
The security system keypad that Flora Ratson sprayed with her special can.

5 **How is this Flora Ratson different?**
The collar of this Flora's shirt is round and pale blue, while the collar of the other Flora's shirt is white and pointy.

6 **What happened onstage?**
Ash Dow is sneaking away.

7 **Rearrange the letters in Ash Dow. What do you get?**
Shadow!

HOW MANY QUESTIONS DID YOU ANSWER CORRECTLY?

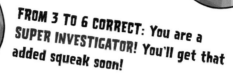

ALL 7 CORRECT: You are a SUPER-SQUEAKY INVESTIGATOR!

FROM 3 TO 6 CORRECT: You are a SUPER INVESTIGATOR! You'll get that added squeak soon!

LESS THAN 3 CORRECT: You are a GOOD INVESTIGATOR! Keep practicing to get super-squeaky!

Farewell until the next mystery!

Geronimo Stilton

Q What do you call a smart group of trees?

A A brainforest.

Q Why did the cookie go to the hospital?

A Cause he was feeling crumby.

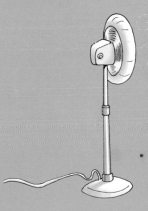

Q Why is it so windy inside a baseball stadium?

A All those fans.

Q How do you catch a whole school of fish?

A With bookworms.

Q **What did one ocean say to the other?**

A Nothing. It just waved.

Q **What did one firefly say to the other?**

A You glow, girl!

Q **What time should you go to the dentist?**

A Tooth hurty.

Q **What did the hat say to the scarf?**

A You hang around, and I'll go ahead.

Q What do you call an old snowman?

A Water!

Q What did the judge say when the skunk walked into the courtroom?

A Odor in the court!

Q What is harder to catch the faster you run?

A Your breath!

Q What does a baby computer call his father?

A Data!

Q  What's the best thing to put into a muffin?

A Your teeth!

Q What makes pirates such good singers?

A They can hit the high Cs!

Q  What kind of flower grows on your face?

A Tulips!

Q What goes up and down but does not move?

A Stairs.